Papa's Home

David Soman

LB

Little, Brown and Company
New York Boston

About This Book

The illustrations for this book were done in watercolor, pen, and ink on Arches 140lb cold-pressed paper. This book was edited by Susan Rich and designed by Camryn Cogshell, with art direction by Saho Fujii. The production was supervised by Patricia Alvarado, and the production editor was Annie McDonnell. The text was set in Gabriela, and the display type is Edith.

• Little, Brown and Company • Hachette Book Group • 1290 Avenue of the Americas, New York, NY 10104 • Visit us at LBYR.com • First Edition: May 2023 • Little, Brown and Company is a division of Hachette Book Group, Inc. • The Little, Brown name and logo are trademarks of Hachette Book Group, Inc. • The publisher is not responsible for websites (or their content) that are not owned by the publisher. • Library of Congress Cataloging-in-Publication Data • Names: Soman, David, author. • Title: Papa's home / David Soman. • Description: First edition. | New York : Little, Brown and Company, 2023. | Audience: Ages 5–8. | Summary: "A child worries about what it will be like while his papa is away, until papa is home"— Provided by publisher. • Identifiers: LCCN 2022030606 (print) | ISBN 9780316427838 • Subjects: CYAC: Separation anxiety—Fiction. | Father and child—Fiction. | LCGFT: Picture books. • Classification: LCC PZ7.S696224 Pap 2023 (print) | DDC [E]—dc23 • LC record available at https://lccn.loc.gov/2022030606 • ISBN 978-0-316-42783-8 • Printed in China • APS • 10 9 8 7 6 5 4 3 2 1

For Sam, grown wise and strong

Papa? Are you up?

I am now.

Is it breakfast time?

It's breakfast waffles time!

Then let's get dressed.

Arms up.

Papa? Are you still going away tomorrow?

I am, but I'll be back before you know it.

And Aunt Jessie will be with me?

The whole time.

What if she wants me to wear
my old yellow rain boots? I
don't want to wear those!

She won't do that.

Well, if she does, I'll run away.

In those boots?

PAPA!

I like blueberry waffles—
what if she puts something
weird in them?

Like what?

Like baloney. 'Cause I won't eat those baloney waffles.

Neither would I.

Are we going to have a picnic in the park today?

Count on it, kiddo.

Ready to go?

YES!

To the playground!

To the playground!

Papa! Look at me!

Now the swing!

Higher!

I like swinging high.

You were way up there.

I used to be scared to do that, but not anymore.

Growing up is like that.

I skipped it! Did you see how far it went?

That was your farthest one yet!

I could show Aunt Jessie how to skip stones,
if she doesn't know how.

I bet you could.

It might be hard for her. It's hard to skip stones on your first try.

I remember.

Getting sleepy, kiddo?

No! Look how high I
can climb this rock.

Catch me!

Papa's got you.

I don't want you to leave!

I know you don't.

I WANT YOU TO STAY HOME!

Hey, hey, it's okay. It's okay. I'm coming back.

Supper's ready!

Papa, this is good spaghetti!

Thank you.

Maybe one day I'll make
spaghetti for you.

I'd like that.

Careful, we don't want to get soap in your eyes.

Does Aunt Jessie know how to wash my ears?

You know it. She gave you baths when you were very little.

I forgot that!

    That's when she gave you Ducky and Tugboat.

I was a baby back then, not like now.

    No, not like now.

Will Aunt Jessie read me books at night?

Yes.

Three books, like you do?

Maybe four, if you ask.

Papa? Will Aunt Jessie tuck me in?

    Of course.

It won't be the same as you.

    No, but it will be nice because
    Aunt Jessie loves you.

But I'll miss you.

Will you miss me?

> So, so much! Know what I'll be
> thinking about the whole time I'm away?

What?

> All the things we do together:
> like eating waffles, playing at
> the playground . . .

And skipping stones?

> Yup.

And bath time?

> Of course!

And reading books to me?

> Especially reading books to you.
> Because being with you is my favorite
> thing, and there is no place I'd rather
> be than home, doing things with you.

Me too!

I love you. Tons.

I love you tons, too.

Papa . . .

Papa's home.